Witch in the House

by RUTH CHEW

Illustrated by the author

SCHOLASTIC BOOK SERVICES
NEW YORK · TORONTO · LONDON · AUCKLAND · SYDNEY · TOKYO

ISBN: 0-590-00093-4

Copyright © 1975 by Ruth Chew. All rights reserved. Published by Scholastic Book Services, a division of Scholastic Magazines, Inc.

13 12 11 10 9 8 7   0 1 2 3 4 5/8

Printed in the U.S.A.   11

To Emma

1

"LAURA, make Charlie come into the house. The neighbors will complain." Mrs. Allen got up from the breakfast table and looked out of the kitchen window.

The fat yellow tomcat was sitting on the top bar of the swings in the yard. He was yowling.

Laura ran out of the house. "Charlie, come down here."

Charlie yowled louder.

Laura went back into the kitchen. She remembered that there were three sardines on a plate in the refrigerator. Laura cut off the tail of one of the sardines and took it into the yard. She held it up to the cat.

Charlie forgot what he was yowling about. He stretched his neck to see what Laura was holding. She waved the fish tail. Charlie caught a whiff of sardine. He jumped to the ground. Laura ran to the back door and opened it. The cat followed her into the house.

"Mother, somebody has been messing with the swings." Laura gave Charlie the sardine tail. Then she filled his bowl with Cat Chow.

"Don't be silly, Laura. No one can get into the yard." Mrs. Allen put the breakfast dishes in the sink.

Laura's father wiped the kitchen table with a dishcloth. "It's late," he said. "We'll have to hurry if we want to get to work on time."

"Load the dishwasher, please, Laura," her mother said. Mrs. Allen found her handbag in the dining room. She took a quick look at herself in the round mirror in the front hall. Then she followed Mr. Allen out the front door.

Laura started to put the dishes into the dishwasher. The doorbell rang. She went to answer it. Her friend Jane Gilbert stood on the front stoop.

"Come in." Laura opened the door wide. "You're just in time to help me load the dishwasher."

Jane stepped into the hall. "I think you save the work till I get here. Yesterday I made the beds for you."

Laura walked into the kitchen. She pulled out a chair for her friend. "Sit down, Jane. You don't have to help if you don't want to."

Jane watched Laura scrape the food off the dishes and stack them in the dishwasher. After about a minute she jumped up from her chair. She grabbed a handful of spoons and knives. "You'll be all day, slowpoke. I want to swing."

When the dishes were all in the dishwasher, Jane and Laura went out into the back yard. Jane looked at the swings. "What were you trying to do, swing double-decker?"

There were two swings. One had been unhooked from the metal bar. The chains of the two swings were tied together. One seat hung over the other.

"I didn't do this," Laura said.

"Who did?" Jane asked.

"I don't know," Laura said. "Somebody must have come into the yard last night. I told Mother, but she thinks nobody can get over the fence."

Jane looked at the tall fence. "It *is* pretty high."

Laura started to untangle the chains. "Give me a hand, Jane."

It took almost half an hour to get the knots out of the chains. Then Laura shinnied up one of the swing poles and

hooked the loose swing back in place. Now the girls could swing.

Laura pumped herself higher and higher. She felt as if she were flying. The swing sailed up almost into the leafy branches of the apple tree overhead.

"Be careful you don't swing over the top bar," Jane said.

Suddenly there was a long low howl. The yellow cat was staring out of the kitchen window at the swings.

Jane let her swing come to a stop. "I'm getting seasick," she said. "And what's wrong with your cat? Do you think he's jealous and wants to swing too?"

"Something really is bothering him," Laura said.

"I almost forgot," Jane said. "Mother told me to ask you to have lunch at my house."

The girls went into the kitchen. Charlie jumped down from the window sill. He ran to rub against Jane's leg.

Laura stared. "He must like you, Jane."

"What's so strange about that?" Jane picked up the cat. Charlie purred and purred.

"He's trying to tell us something," Laura said.

"I told you," Jane scratched the cat behind the ears. "He wants to swing."

2

LAURA went to Jane's house for lunch. Jane's mother served the girls big plates of spaghetti and meat balls. They had watermelon for dessert.

When the meal was over Jane and Laura lay down on the living room rug. "I'm stuffed," Jane said.

"Me too." Laura closed her eyes.

Just then Mrs. Gilbert rushed into the room. She was holding a calendar. "Oh, dear!"

Jane sat up. "What's the matter, Mom?"

"I forgot that you have to go to the dentist this afternoon," Mrs. Gilbert said.

"Why?" Jane asked. "My teeth don't hurt."

"You're due for a check-up. And your teeth need cleaning," her mother said. "We have to leave right away, Jane."

Laura got to her feet. "Thank you for the lunch, Mrs. Gilbert. See you tomorrow, Jane. I hope you don't need any fillings."

Laura's house was four doors down the block from Jane's. She walked slowly home. When she opened her front door she looked for Charlie. The cat usually came running to greet her.

Laura went through the house to the kitchen. The cat was sitting by the back door. Laura opened it. "Remember, Charlie," she said, "no noise!"

The cat streaked out the open door. Laura followed him into the yard. Charlie ran to the swings. He leaped onto the seat of one of them. Laura stared.

Once more the chains were all tangled together. One seat was above the other. Charlie was on the bottom seat. Someone was sitting on the seat over his.

It was an old woman. And she was upside-down!

3

LAURA was too surprised to say a word. She just kept looking at the old woman. Now she saw that the woman's clothes and hair were as neat as if she were right-side-up. Her long black skirt fluttered as she swung back and forth. But it stayed over her knees. She had straight gray hair under a tall black hat. The hat was pointing straight down, but it didn't fall off the old woman's head.

The striped yellow cat sat on the seat under the one the woman was using. His tail stretched out behind him. His eyes were half closed.

Jane was right. Charlie did want to swing.

Laura felt she had to say something. She swallowed hard. Then, in a loud voice, she said, "Excuse me. I think you've made a mistake."

The old woman stopped pumping. She let the swing come to a stop. Then she turned to look at Laura. "Mistake?" she said. "What is it this time?"

"This isn't a public playground," Laura said. "Those are my swings. And I don't like what you're doing to them."

"I'm sorry," the old woman said. "The cat told me I could swing if I gave him a ride." She tipped her head to look at Charlie. He was under her, but she seemed to look up at him. She shook her finger at the cat. "I can't trust anybody these days. And it was such fun swinging." The old woman sighed. She slipped off the swing. But she slipped up, not down. Her feet touched the top bar of the swing set. She seemed to be standing on the bar with her feet up and her head down.

The old woman smoothed her skirt. She walked along the bar. When she came to the end of it she stepped onto a branch of the apple tree. Still upside-down, she walked to the telephone wire.

Oh, Laura thought, she's going to walk tight-rope. But if she falls off she'll shoot into space like a rocket. "Stop!" she called to the old woman. "Come back. You can use my swings if you want to."

The old woman was so startled she almost did fall off the wire. She grabbed it with her hands and crawled back to the tree. When she reached the safety of a large branch she stopped to catch her breath.

Laura stood under the tree and looked up. "Why don't you walk right-side-up?" she asked.

"Can't," the old woman said. She sat on a branch among the little green apples. Her head was down and her feet were up.

"Have you always been like this?" Laura wanted to know.

"Oh, no. Yesterday I was just like everybody else," the old woman told her.

"What happened?" Laura asked.

"I'm not sure," the old woman said. "But I think it's something to do with the swing."

"Meow!" The striped yellow cat was still sitting on the bottom swing.

Laura gave the swing a push. The cat swung high in the air. The breeze blew back his ears and whiskers.

"Cats love to fly," the old woman said.

Laura had been staring hard at her. "Charlie's the wrong color for you," she said. "You're a witch!"

"Now, now. Don't start using bad names," the old woman said. "We were just getting to be friends."

"But you are a witch, aren't you?" Laura persisted.

"Some people say so. But that's such a harsh word. I have always thought of myself as a wise woman. Only now I don't seem so wise anymore."

The breeze rustled the branches of the apple tree. The witch poked her feet into the green leaves. "This is fun," she said.

A moment later she slipped and had to grab hold of the branch.

Laura screamed. "Be careful! Maybe you'd better come into the house. You'd be safer there. I'll get a rope."

Laura remembered that her mother had a length of clothesline in the basement. Mrs. Allen used it when the clothes dryer was out of order. Laura went to get the clothesline. When she came back she found that the witch had slipped off the branch again. She was clinging to it with both hands.

"Hang on!" Laura tied one end of the clothesline to the knob on the back door. "Now catch!" She tossed the other end to the witch.

The old woman grabbed the rope. Then she went crashing up through the tree branches. In a few seconds the witch was above the tree. She was still holding onto the clothesline. The back door shook as if it would come off its hinges.

The witch floated overhead like a kite on a string. Laura grabbed the rope. She pulled as hard as she could. But the witch was too heavy for her.

"I can't get you down," Laura panted. "What shall we do?"

The witch began to shinny down the rope. When she got to the bottom she grabbed the door-knob. "Quick, let me in," she puffed.

Laura opened the door and pulled the witch into the house. The old woman fell to the ceiling with a thump. She lay there, all tired out.

"Poor thing," Laura said to herself. Then she began to think what her mother would say when she came home to find a witch in her kitchen.

4

LAURA looked up at the witch. She seemed to be falling asleep. "I don't think my mother would want you in the kitchen," Laura said. "You can sleep in my closet."

The witch opened her eyes and sat up. "You're very kind," she said. "What's your name?"

"Laura. What's yours?"

"People call me Sally," the old woman said. "It's not really my name, but my name is so long that I can hardly remember it. Lately, I can't seem to remember anything. Where is this closet of yours?"

"Upstairs," Laura said.

"That may cause problems, but we may as well try." The witch stood up and walked across the ceiling to the doorway of the dining room.

Laura lived in an old house with high ceilings. This gave Sally plenty of head room. She didn't have to worry about bumping into the furniture. The biggest problem was the stairs. The only way she could get upstairs was by jumping from one floor to the next.

Laura went to get the clothesline. She threw one end to the witch. Sally looped it around her waist. Laura tied the other end to the bannister rail at the top of the stairs. Together they floated Sally to the ceiling of the upstairs hall.

Laura pointed. "My room is the one at the end of the hall."

The witch untied the clothesline and walked to Laura's bedroom. Laura opened the closet door and turned on

the light. "I think there's enough room for you in here."

Sally walked across the ceiling and climbed into the closet. She looked around. "It's cozy," she said.

Laura didn't think the ceiling would be a comfortable bed. She took an old quilt out of the linen closet and handed it to the witch.

Just then Laura heard the front door open. Her mother and father had come home. Laura put her finger to her lips. "Go to sleep, Sally," she whispered. "I'll be back later."

The witch curled up on the quilt in the corner of the closet. Laura turned out the light and shut the closet door. She went downstairs to greet her parents.

5

IT WASN'T until the kitchen was all cleaned up after supper that Laura remembered that the witch might be hungry. Her mother and father were watching a movie on television in the living room. Laura opened the refrigerator. She found chicken wings left over from supper and some chunks of fresh pineapple. Laura put these on a plate along with two slices of buttered bread. She took the plate upstairs to the witch.

Sally was asleep. When Laura turned on the light in the closet she opened her eyes. She yawned and stretched.

"I brought you something to eat." Laura held up the plate. "Be careful how you take it."

The witch craned her neck to see what Laura had brought. "I'm afraid that would make me sick, dear," she said. "Don't you have any bones? Oh, and if you have the shell of the pineapple, that would be just fine."

"I'll see what I can find." Laura tiptoed back downstairs with the plate of food.

There was still one quarter of the pineapple in the refrigerator. Laura took the piece of shell and left the chunks of fruit. She started to pull the bones out of the chicken wings.

"Meow." Charlie rubbed against her legs.

"No, Charlie. Bones are bad for you." Laura dropped the chicken bones and the pineapple rind into a little plastic bag. This would be easier to hide than the plate. And the witch wouldn't have to be so careful holding it.

"Meow." Charlie rubbed against her legs again. Laura gave him the meat she had taken off the bones. Suddenly she had an idea. She dumped a spoonful of something from the sink into the plastic bag. Then she hurried back upstairs.

Sally was delighted. She bit into the prickly pineapple shell with her sharp pointed teeth. "Delicious!" she said. "And what a wonderful flavor these crunchy little brown things have! I haven't tasted anything so good in ages."

Laura nodded her head. "I had a hunch you'd like wet coffee grounds."

6

"ISN'T your witch good for anything?" Jane asked. "Of course, I guess it's fun to have a witch hanging upside-down like a bat in your closet. And it must be interesting to figure out what to feed her. What did she eat for breakfast?"

"Burnt toast and eggshells," Laura told her.

The two girls were sitting on Laura's front stoop. Mr. and Mrs. Allen had gone to work. Laura wanted to tell Jane all about Sally before she took her into the house to meet the witch.

"Maybe she can cast spells that will do the housework," Jane suggested.

"She's pretty absent-minded," Laura said. "I think she'd make a mess of any spell she tried."

Jane thought about this. "Maybe you're right. Instead of making themselves, the beds might disappear."

"That reminds me," Laura said. "I haven't made the beds yet." She got up and opened the front door. "Come on in, Jane."

They found the witch in the bathroom. She had turned the shower-head to point straight up and was sitting on the ceiling taking a shower. Her clothes were folded in a corner of the ceiling. They didn't seem to have anything holding them up.

When Laura and Jane came into the room Sally stood on tiptoe to turn off the water. "Would you hand me a towel, dear," she said to Laura.

Laura went to get a towel from the linen closet down the hall. She held it up to the witch. Sally reached out of the shower door to take the towel. She wrapped herself in it and stepped out of the shower stall.

"This is my friend Jane," Laura said.

Jane looked up at the dripping witch. "How do you do?"

"Fine, thank you," the witch replied. "Could you just hand me that bath mat, please. And now, if you'll excuse me a moment, I'd like to get dressed."

Laura picked up the pink bath mat from the floor and gave it to the witch. Then she and Jane went to make the beds. They peeped into the closet in Laura's room. Sally had folded the quilt and put it on the shelf above the clothes pole.

"I always thought witches were dirty," Jane said.

Laura fluffed her pillow and put the spread on her bed. "I'm not sure her taking showers upside-down is good for the bathroom ceiling."

"Maybe you could persuade her to wash with a damp washcloth," Jane said.

"That's a good idea," they heard the witch say. "I'm sorry I didn't think of it." Sally was climbing over the wall above the doorway. She walked across the ceiling and looked out of the tall bay windows. "It's a lovely day. I wish I could go out. If I could gather a few things in your garden I might be able to mix up a brew."

"What would you cook it on?" Jane asked. "You'd burn the house down if you made a fire on the ceiling."

Sally wrinkled her forehead. "I forgot about that," she said. Then she smiled. "I know a recipe for cold brew. We could try that."

Jane thought for a minute. "Maybe Laura and I could get the things for you to use in the brew," she said.

Laura went to get her father's field glasses. She handed them to the witch. "Look through these and see if you can find what you need in the garden."

Sally held the glasses to her eyes. She looked out of the window. "Aphids," she said. "Not good enough. Rose thorns. Better." She began to get excited. "There's a slug! Now, if I had a teensy bit of poison ivy —"

Laura interrupted her. "Sally, don't you know any spells you can do by rubbing a lamp or waving a wand?"

Witch Sally put the field glasses on top of the window frame. She took off her tall black hat and scratched her head. "I know one I can do with an umbrella," she said. "But I've forgotten just what it does."

Laura ran downstairs. She found her father's big black umbrella hanging on a hook in the hall closet. She carried it upstairs and handed it to the witch.

Sally waved the umbrella three times around her head and said something like "crocodile tears." Then she opened the umbrella.

There was a flash of lightning and a loud crash of thunder. The whole house seemed to shake. Outside the sky grew dark. The rain began to pour down.

"Oh," Sally said, "that's what it does."

"Turn it off," Jane said.

"I've forgotten how," the witch told her.

"Well, anyway, now we can't gather slugs in the garden." Laura closed the window. "We'll have to think of some rainy-day magic instead."

7

"I'D BETTER shut the windows downstairs." Laura ran out of the room.

Jane picked up the umbrella and closed it. Instantly the rain stopped. A gust of wind blew the clouds away. The next moment the room was filled with sunshine. Jane stared at the umbrella. "That's quite a trick," she said. "Will it work with any umbrella?"

"Not with the kind with springs in them or made of plastic," the witch told her. Sally was once more looking out of the window with the field glasses. "Ah," she said, "caterpillars!"

Jane decided to take the umbrella downstairs. She met Laura in the front hall. "Your witch wants caterpillars now," Jane said.

"Ick!" Laura took the umbrella. "That was a short storm."

"It stopped as soon as I closed the umbrella," Jane said.

"I'd rather have a spell that stopped rain when you wanted to go to the beach or something." Laura hung the umbrella back on the hook in the hall closet. "Come on back upstairs, Jane. I'd better straighten up the bathroom."

The ceiling over the shower stall was still wet. The bath mat was stuck to the ceiling. Laura went to ask the witch to take it off.

Sally was looking through the field glasses. She put them down when Laura came into the room. "Do you have a pencil and paper, dear? I'll make a list of what I need. If you can't find a toad, a frog or even a tadpole might do."

"I'll get you a pencil later, Sally,"

Laura said. "Right now could you take the mat off the bathroom ceiling?"

"You don't understand, dear," the witch said. "If I don't write the list now I'll forget part of it. Now, what was it I said I needed?"

Laura found an old school notebook on top of her desk. She tore out a page and gave it to the witch with a pencil stub. Then she left the room.

There was an aluminum stepladder in the basement. Laura went to get it. Her mother and father would be sure to ask why the bath mat was on the ceiling. Laura didn't want to forget the bath mat any more than the witch wanted to forget her list.

Laura put the ladder in the stall shower. Jane held it steady while Laura climbed up and dried the ceiling with a towel. Together the girls moved the stepladder under the bath mat. This time Laura held the ladder and Jane climbed up.

Jane pulled at the bath mat. It fell halfway to the floor. Then it stopped and floated in the air. Jane poked it with her finger. She yanked at one corner. The pink bath mat wobbled a little, but it stayed where it was.

"Laura," Jane whispered, "your nutty witch has done something to it. I can't get it down."

Laura was staring up at the mat. "From here it looks just like a flying carpet," she said.

"It does from here too," Jane agreed. She kept hold of the stepladder with one hand and slid over so that she was sitting on the bath mat.

Laura watched her. "Aren't you afraid you'll fall off, Jane?"

"It feels steady," Jane said. "Now, if we could just figure out how to work it —"

"You mean you want to fly on it?" Laura asked.

"Of course. Don't you?" Jane let go of the ladder. She sat cross-legged on the bath mat. "If we sit close together there's room for both of us."

"In the stories you just have to talk to flying carpets," Laura said.

"OK," Jane said. "Here goes. Bath mat, please fly down to the floor."

The bath mat gave a little shake. Jane held tight to the edges. Then the mat floated down to the bathroom floor. Jane stood up and stepped off. She closed the bathroom door. "Laura," she whispered, "why do you think the witch did this?"

"I don't know," Laura said, "but the way that mat was in mid-air she could sit on it upside-down."

"She could fly out of the window at night and back without your knowing," Jane said. "I don't trust her. After all, she is a witch. Laura, you don't have to tell her we know the bath mat is enchanted. After all, it isn't her mat. It's yours."

Laura folded the bath mat and went to hide it in the linen closet.

8

SALLY was still sitting on the ceiling by the window. She was sucking the end of the pencil stub. When Laura and Jane came into the room she held out the sheet of paper. "I made a list of things to use in a simple cold brew. Do you think you could get these?"

Laura took the paper and read aloud:

> 1 live frog, toad, or 3 good-sized tadpoles
> ½ tablespoonful of ground glass
> 1 cup of swamp water
> 1 jellyfish
> 1 sprig fresh poison ivy

"Are you sure you need *all* this stuff, Sally?"

"Let me see the list," Jane said.

Laura handed it to her.

"1 sprig fresh poison ivy," Jane read. "Sally," she said, "I can't go *near* poison ivy!" She gave the list back to Laura. Laura folded it and stuffed it into the pocket of her jeans.

The witch stroked her chin and thought hard. "We could use wolfsbane instead of poison ivy," she said. "Now, what was it you wanted me to do for you before I wrote the list?"

"Nothing," Laura told her. "What are you going to use the brew for, Sally?"

"I'm tired of being upside-down," the old woman said. "Maybe the brew will cure me."

"Couldn't you do other magic with it too?" Jane asked.

"Of course," the witch said. "I used to be a whizz at granting wishes."

"Meow." The yellow cat walked into the room. He tipped his head to look at the witch and let out a yowl.

"I'm sorry I can't take you swinging," Sally told him.

Laura had an idea. "Charlie, do you know where there's any wolfsbane?"

The cat purred.

"He says it's all over the place," Sally told the girls. "Why don't you take the cat along with you and let him point it out?"

"Come on, Charlie," Jane said. "I'll take you swinging." She picked up the cat and went downstairs and out into the yard.

Laura was left alone with the witch. "Are you sure you won't mind being by yourself while Jane and I go to collect the things for your brew?"

"No, no, dear," Sally said. "I'll be all right as long as I have a good book."

Laura handed her a book of magic tricks. It seemed like something a witch would like. She had taken it out of the

library two days before. "There's a good one about putting an egg into a bottle," she said.

The old woman lay on her stomach near the window to read. Laura went to join Jane.

9

JANE and Charlie were both swinging when Laura walked out into the back yard. Jane sat on the bottom swing. Charlie was on the one over her head.

"Keep your tail out of my eyes, cat," Jane said. "Laura, this cat isn't too bright. I'm not sure I want him along when we go looking for tadpoles."

"How will we find the wolfsbane without him?" Laura wanted to know. "We'll have to get started if we're going to get all this stuff."

"I'd better tell Mom I won't be home for a while," Jane said. "Where shall I say we're going?"

"The Botanic Garden," Laura told her.

"That seems like the place to look for wolfsbane."

"They have a NO DOGS sign on the gate there. But it doesn't say anything about cats." Jane stopped swinging. Charlie stayed on his seat and yowled.

"Stop fussing, Charlie," Laura whispered to the cat. "If you like flying you're going to have fun."

While Jane ran home to talk to her mother, Laura went quietly upstairs to get the bath mat. She took it out of the linen closet and rolled it up. When Jane came back, Laura was waiting on the front steps with the mat under one arm and the cat under the other.

Jane was carrying a big shopping bag.

"What do you have in there?" Laura asked.

"Plastic bags and peanut butter jars," Jane said. "We have to have something to bring the stuff home in. Oh, and Mom gave me some sandwiches. She's going shopping. She thought it would be a good idea if I ate lunch out."

"There's a NO PICNICKING sign in the Botanic Garden," Laura said.

"Prospect Park is right across the street from there," Jane reminded her. "We'll get the wolfsbane first and then eat in the park."

Laura unrolled the pink bath mat on the stoop. She sat down cross-legged on it and held the cat in her lap. Jane sat down with her back against Laura's. There was just enough room for the two of them.

"Bath mat," Laura said, "please take us to the Botanic Garden."

The bath mat began to feel stiff under her. Laura held her breath. She could feel her heart pounding. She kept a tight hold on Charlie with one hand and grabbed the side of the mat with the other.

Jane held the handles of the shopping bag in her teeth. She clung to the sides of the bath mat with both hands.

The mat slid off the front stoop of Laura's house. It began to rise straight up in the air like an elevator. Higher and higher it went until it could skim over the roof of the tallest apartment building. Two old men on the corner of the street didn't notice a thing. They went right on talking to each other.

At first Jane and Laura were too scared to look down. But the bath mat was so steady that Laura finally stretched her neck and peeped over the edge. "We're flying right over our school."

Jane took the shopping bag handles out of her mouth. "Too bad school is

closed for the summer. It would be great
to have Mrs. Sanders look up and see us
flying overhead."

"If school were open we'd be in it,"
Laura said.

Charlie sat quite still in Laura's lap.
His eyes got bigger and bigger.

The bath mat didn't seem to be going fast, but in almost no time they were over the park. Then they sailed above Flatbush Avenue. Now they were going straight down. The mat landed on a grassy slope in the Botanic Garden. People were walking along a winding path. They were busy looking at the flowers and never saw the two girls and the yellow cat drop out of the sky.

Laura and Jane stood up and stepped onto the grass. Laura put Charlie on the ground and rolled up the bath mat.

"Oh, look," Jane said. "There's a rabbit. I didn't know there were any here."

10

CHARLIE saw the rabbit too. He streaked across the grass after it. The next minute he was playing hide and seek in a bed of pansies. The little rabbit stood still and tried to pretend he was a lump of dirt. The cat knew better. He was about to pounce.

"Oh, the poor little rabbit," Jane said.

Suddenly Laura had an idea. She unrolled the bath mat. "Mat," she said, "bring me my cat."

This time the bath mat didn't make itself stiff. It flew across the grass and flopped down over the yellow cat. Then it folded itself around the cat and sailed back to Laura. She held out her arms. The bath mat snuggled into them.

Laura unfolded one corner of the mat and looked into Charlie's surprised face. "If you don't get busy and find us some wolfsbane, I'll take you home."

Charlie yawned.

This time someone had noticed the bath mat. A man who was raking a flower bed walked over to the two girls. Laura covered Charlie's face with the bath mat.

"Don't you know better than to throw things into the pansies?" the man said to Laura. "Two of the plants are crushed. I'll have to ask you to leave the Garden." He made the girls go with him to the nearest gate. And he watched while they walked through the turnstile.

Laura kept the cat hidden in the bath

mat. Charlie stayed quiet. They were walking along Flatbush Avenue.

"If I didn't know Charlie I'd think he was sorry for what he did," Laura said. "What do we do now?"

"Go back into the Garden by a different gate," Jane said.

The girls walked around the corner. There was another entrance to the Garden near the parking lot of the Brooklyn Museum. They went in that one.

The Garden was full of squirrels. Laura was sure Charlie would chase them. He couldn't help it. And now they had to make sure that the man who made them leave the Garden didn't see them.

It was some time before Laura unwrapped the cat and put him on the ground again. Charlie trotted along the walks, sniffing the plants. He started to chew one.

"Catnip!" Laura said. "Get him away from that. He'll go crazy." She snatched the cat up in her arms and carried him until he'd forgotten the catnip. Then she put him down again.

"I'm getting hungry," Jane said. "And I don't think that cat is ever going to find any wolfsbane."

"Meow!" Charlie ran over to a tall plant with yellow flowers.

"Wolfsbane, Charlie?" Laura asked.

"Meow." Charlie curled his tail around the stem of the plant.

Jane looked to be sure no one was watching. Then she broke off a little sprig of the flowers. She carefully put it into one of the plastic bags she had in her shopping bag. "Now, let's go eat lunch."

11

LAURA bit into a sandwich. "Tuna fish!" She gave Charlie some of hers. He tried to catch a squirrel while the girls finished their lunch. Mrs. Gilbert had packed two peaches in with the sandwiches. Jane and Laura each took a long drink of water from the drinking fountain in the park.

Jane wiped her mouth with the back of her hand. "Now, let's see the list."

Laura pulled the paper out of her pocket and unfolded it. "Ground glass," she said. "There are a lot of broken bottles here in the park."

"And that nutty witch can just chew them a bit to grind them up," Jane said. She picked up several pieces of green glass from a pile near one of the benches. Jane packed them in the brown paper bag that had held the sandwiches. She put it in the bottom of her shopping bag.

Laura looked at the list again. "Swamp water and tadpoles. I wonder if lake water would do. It smells pretty bad."

The girls walked over to the lake in the park. Jane filled one of her peanut butter jars with lake water. People were fishing in the lake. One boy had caught two sunfish. Jane asked him about tadpoles.

"I've never seen them here," the boy said. "It's too late in the summer for them anyway."

"What about frogs?" Laura wanted to know.

"I know where you can find them."
The boy put a piece of bread on his
hook. He tossed the hook into the lake.
"But you mustn't let anybody see you
catch them. And you may have to sneak
in the gate. The guards don't want kids
in the place. If you can't get in the gate
there are some wide spaces in the fence."

"What's this place you're talking
about?" Jane asked.

"Greenwood Cemetery," the boy said.

"Oh, that's on the other side of McDonald Avenue." Laura picked up the cat. "My father says it's bigger than this park."

The boy dragged his line through the water. "Watch out for the dogs in the cemetery. They keep big ones there."

Laura decided to take the cat home.

Jane and Laura left the lake and climbed a hill. At the top was a grassy place with woods all around. Here they spread out the bath mat and sat down on it. Charlie curled up in Laura's lap. Jane held tight to the shopping bag.

"Mat," Laura said, "please take us home."

The pink bath mat stiffened itself. It quivered for a second. Then it rose until it was high over the trees. It made a half-turn and sailed away from the park and over the roofs of Brooklyn.

12

THE bath mat touched down on Laura's front stoop.

Jane stood up and stretched. "I wonder what time it is."

Laura stepped off the mat. "We'll look at the kitchen clock." She opened her front door. "Come in, Jane."

Charlie ran into the house. Laura picked up the bath mat and folded it. The two girls went into the kitchen. It was after four o'clock.

"Too late to go to the cemetery," Jane said. "My mother ought to be finished with her shopping by now."

"And Sally hasn't had any lunch." Laura felt guilty. "What shall I feed her."

"Try lake water and broken glass," Jane suggested. She put her shopping bag on the kitchen table. "I'd better go home, Laura. See you tomorrow."

After Jane had gone, Laura took the shopping bag upstairs. Sally was in the closet. "Is that you, dear?" she called in a sleepy voice when Laura came into her room. "I just had a lovely nap."

"Sally," Laura said, "suppose it was my mother and not me."

Sally thought about this. She noticed the bath mat. It was still tucked under Laura's arm. "I see you got your mat off the ceiling."

"Yes," Laura said. "You did a nice job of enchanting it, Sally."

The witch looked surprised. "What do you mean?"

"It flies very well. Jane and I went to the Botanic Garden with it." Laura gave the mat a little hug. "And it stopped

Charlie from catching a baby rabbit."
She looked at the bath mat. "Oh, Sally!
It has grass stains on it. Will it spoil the
magic to wash it?"

"I don't know," Sally said. "To tell
the truth, I didn't know I enchanted it.
I must have done something to it, but
I can't think what."

Laura remembered the things in the
shopping bag. She took out the paper
bag with the green glass in it.

Sally took one look at the glass and
smacked her lips. "Yum!" she said. "Now
that I think of it, I really am hungry."
She licked a corner of one of the bits of
glass. It seemed to melt like a lollipop.

Jane was right. Sally did like to eat broken glass. Laura fished the jar of lake water out of the shopping bag. She took off the lid.

The witch sniffed the air. "What do you have in that jar, dear?"

"Lake water," Laura said. "We thought it might take the place of swamp water in your recipe."

"Most lake water wouldn't, but this seems rather special," Sally told her.

Laura held her nose. She handed the

jar to the old woman. The glass Sally was licking was almost gone.

"Oh please save some of that for the ground glass in the recipe," Laura said.

"Oh, that's right," the witch said. "I forgot."

Laura reached into the shopping bag and brought out the plastic bag with the sprig of yellow flowers in it. "Here's the wolfsbane."

The witch drew her shaggy eyebrows together. "Wolfsbane? Oh yes. We need it for the cold brew. But those are the *flowers*. What we need is the *root*."

"I had a lot of trouble getting the flowers," Laura said. "I'm sure nobody in the Botanic Garden would let me pull up a plant, root and all."

Sally was sipping the lake water. "If only I could go with you," she said, "I'm sure I could find some more wolfsbane. Those flowers grow everywhere."

13

JANE and Laura were swinging. It had taken them a long time to untangle the swing chains. Charlie climbed up into the apple tree to watch. Jane looked at him. "I know," she said, "you liked the swings better when they were one above the other. Well, it's you or me, cat." Jane pumped the swing higher.

"I wish we could take Sally along when we go to get the other things for the brew," Laura said.

"I'll bet that witch just loves grave-yards." Jane zoomed up into the air. "Laura, you never should have told her about the magic bath mat."

"I thought she knew it was enchanted."

Laura let her swing coast to a stop. "Who ever heard of an absent-minded witch?"

"Nobody." Jane swung higher. "Didn't you ever think that she's not absent-minded at all? She's just fooling you."

"I don't care," Laura said. "I feel sorry for her cooped up in that closet. I'd like to take her for a ride on the bath mat."

"There's only enough room for the two of us," Jane said, "unless the witch rides upside-down underneath the mat."

"That's the only way she could ride," Laura said. "Of course, we might have trouble getting on and off the mat."

Now Jane was interested. She enjoyed solving problems. "We could get on first," she said. "And then you could tell Pinky to rise high enough for the witch to slide under him."

"*Pinky?*" Laura said. "It does seem nicer than calling him *Mat*. Do you think he'd like to be called Pinky?"

"There's one way to find out." Jane let her swing die. She jumped off and ran into the house. Laura followed her.

The two girls raced upstairs. Laura pulled the bath mat out of the back of the linen closet where she had hidden it. She unfolded the mat and put it on the floor of the upstairs hall. "Flip one corner for *yes* and two for *no*," she told the bath mat. "Would you like to be called *Pinky* instead of *Mat*?"

The bath mat waved one corner.

"That settles it. We'll call him Pinky." Jane sat down on the floor beside the bath mat. "Pinky," she said, "could you fly with Laura and me on top of you and Witch Sally underneath?"

The mat was still for a minute, as if

it were thinking. Then, slowly, it flipped a corner.

"What a lovely idea!" Witch Sally stepped over the wall at the doorway of Laura's room. She walked along the ceiling of the hall toward the two girls. "I couldn't help hearing you, Jane. I think you would make a very clever witch. Have you ever thought of going into the trade?"

14

"LAURA, I hope you have something to pack for Sally's lunch. If you don't, she'll eat the frogs." Jane was making peanut butter sandwiches.

Laura mixed bottled lemon juice with water and sugar. She took a tray of ice cubes out of the refrigerator. "I saved all the cobs from the corn we had for dinner last night and the rind from the grapefruit Daddy ate at breakfast. If I season the stuff with wet coffee grounds Sally will eat it." Laura poured her lemonade into a thermos bottle. Then she put the witch's lunch into a plastic bag.

Laura went upstairs to get the shopping bag from her bedroom. Sally was sitting on the ceiling looking out of the window. "It will be good to get outdoors for a change," she said.

The bath mat was folded up on Laura's bed. Laura picked it up and handed it to the witch. "Do you think you could ride downstairs?"

Sally spread the mat on the ceiling and sat down on it. The old woman was so excited that her voice trembled. "Pinky," she said. "Please take me down to the kitchen."

The bath mat stiffened and began to skim along, an inch or two below the ceiling. Sally sat straight. Her black hat pointed at the floor. Her eyes shone under her shaggy eyebrows. The mat sailed down the hallway.

Laura called after it. "Be careful not to bang her head on the stairs, Pinky."

The witch arrived safely in the kitchen. Jane looked up at her. "I think

Laura and I could climb aboard from the swing chains." She opened the back door. "Come on, Pinky. This is the hard part."

The bath mat flew out into the yard. It hovered between the two swings. Laura and Jane had tucked the lunch into the shopping bag along with the peanut butter jars and the plastic bags. Laura held the shopping bag while Jane climbed up a swing chain and crawled onto the bath mat. Laura stood on a swing and handed Jane the shopping bag. Then she climbed up to sit beside her on the mat.

"Meow!" The cat was still in the apple tree.

"I can't take you, Charlie," Laura said. "You wouldn't like the dogs." Laura grabbed hold of the edges of the bath mat. "Pinky," she said, "please take us to Greenwood Cemetery."

15

THE bath mat flew high over the tall iron fence. Laura and Jane looked down on a big old house. It was built of brownstone and had square towers and fancy chimneys. A guard stood beside the gate of the cemetery. He didn't look up.

There were hills covered with huge trees. There were statues and tombstones in the shade of the trees. The girls saw strange little stone houses and doorways going into the hills. Winding roads led through the cemetery.

Pinky felt firm and solid under them. There was no sound from the witch. Jane and Laura could see the fluttering of her black skirt. It trailed behind the bath mat.

Now they were flying over a little lake. "Stop, Pinky," Jane said. "This looks like a good place to find frogs."

The bath mat stopped still in mid-air.

Laura leaned over the edge to look at Sally. "You'd better stay under the mat. Jane and I can get off to look for frogs."

"Fine," the witch agreed.

"Pinky," Jane said. "Let us off on that tree." She pointed to it.

The bath mat dropped down until it was close beside a weeping willow tree. Jane and Laura scrambled onto a thick branch. Laura climbed down to the ground first. "Hand me the shopping bag, Jane." She reached up for it.

Sally lay down under the mat. It was not long enough. Her legs stuck out over the end. "I think I'll take a little snooze," she said. "Wake me if you want any help." She closed her eyes. The bath mat floated in the air near the weeping willow.

Laura and Jane took a peanut butter jar out of the shopping bag. They left the shopping bag under the willow tree and walked across the soft green grass to the marshy bank of the little lake. The water was so still they could see clouds reflected in it. Pink and white water lilies floated near the shore.

Jane grabbed Laura's arm. She pointed to a lily pad. A big green frog sat on it and blinked at them.

Laura took the lid off the peanut butter jar and inched toward the frog. She lifted the jar to bring it down over the frog.

Plop! The frog dived into the water.

Jane saw another frog. He was hiding in the water just at the edge of the lake. She cupped her hands and made a dive for him. "Got him," Jane said.

Laura held the jar for Jane to put the frog in. Just as she was ready to put on the lid, the frog gave a leap. He flipped out of the jar and did a back somersault onto the grass. With three hops he was back in the water.

The sun was hot. Laura and Jane sat at the edge of the water for a long time. All the frogs seemed to be hiding. A shadow fell across the grass beside the girls. Laura looked up.

The bath mat had floated over to them. Witch Sally was lying under it. She looked cool in the shade of the mat. Sally smiled. Her stiff gray hair stuck out in little points from under her hat. She wiggled her toes. "Croak," the witch said.

The girls heard an answering croak from the bank of the lake. A small frog was sitting there taking a sunbath. At once Pinky dipped down over the frog.

The witch reached out and grabbed him by the hind leg. "Where's your jar, Jane?"

Jane picked up the jar from where Laura had dropped it on the grass. She popped it over the frog Sally was holding. Laura screwed on the lid. She had made four nail holes in it before they left home. The little frog was caught. Laura felt sorry for him.

Jane saw Sally look at the frog and lick her lips. Jane grabbed the peanut butter jar and raced up the grassy bank to the willow tree. She took the sandwiches and the witch's lunch out of the shopping bag. "Time to eat!" she yelled.

16

SALLY crawled off the bath mat onto a branch of the willow tree to eat her lunch. Laura climbed into the tree to get to the mat. She rolled him up and tucked him under her arm. She was afraid Pinky would wander off. And she wasn't sure he would come if she whistled.

Laura looked down. A huge dog was racing toward the tree. "Watch out, Jane!"

Jane was sitting under the tree. She turned and saw the dog. Jumping to her feet, Jane grabbed hold of a vine that hung down from a branch. She swung herself up into the tree. The dog grabbed the end of her pants leg and wouldn't let go.

"Quick," the witch said, "unroll the bath mat."

Laura gave the mat a shake. It unrolled in mid-air and stayed still while the witch crawled under it.

"Pinky," Sally said, "let's play tag."

The bath mat dropped down so that Sally could pull the dog's tail. The dog let go of Jane's pants leg. Jane climbed higher in the tree. Now the mat dodged back and forth. The witch tweaked the dog's ears and patted his back. All the time she led him farther from the tree. At last the mat and the witch led the dog over the top of a hill and out of sight.

"That was close," Laura said. "Did he hurt you, Jane?"

Jane was looking at the leg of her pants. "I'm all right. But there are some holes from his teeth in my jeans."

Laura handed Jane a sandwich. "Let's eat before anything else happens."

Jane took a bite. "The weather's changing. It's going to rain. Where do you suppose that witch is?"

"Do you think the dog caught her?" Laura asked.

"No. I think she's decided to take off with your bath mat," Jane said.

Laura poured herself a drink of lemonade. "She wants to make that brew to turn herself right-side-up. And we've got almost everything she needs for it."

Laura pointed to a pink spot in the sky. It was getting bigger. The bath mat was coming back.

Pinky sailed up to the tree. The witch was still sitting under him. She waved a handful of leaves and flowers and roots. "Wolfsbane!"

Jane took a good look at the plant. "You mean *buttercups*."

"Same family," Sally said. "They'll work just as well." She crawled off the mat into the tree and looked to see what sort of lunch Laura had packed for her.

Dark clouds were gathering. Jane began to cram things into the shopping bag. "I wish you knew a spell to stop rain instead of just one to start it."

The witch took a bite of corncob. "A little rain never hurt anyone."

A drop splashed on Laura's nose. "Do you think you could eat your lunch on the way home, Sally?"

Sally crunched and swallowed. "It might even taste better that way."

Laura was already on the mat. She moved over for Jane to sit down. Sally made herself comfortable underneath the mat. Jane checked to make sure they had the thermos bottle, the buttercups, and the frog. "OK, Pinky, take us home."

17

THE rain began to come down hard. Jane and Laura were both soaking wet when they got home. Sally was dry. She had been under the bath mat.

Jane went home to change her clothes.

Pinky was so wet he could hardly flip his corners. He had mud stains as well as grass stains on him now. He seemed like a friend to Laura. She didn't like to think of him being banged around in the washing machine or the dryer. Instead she gave him a warm bath in the tub and hung him in the stall shower to drip dry. Then she went to talk to the witch.

Sally was all worn out from the trip to the cemetery. She was curled up on the quilt in the corner of Laura's closet. And she was snoring.

Laura closed the closet door and went downstairs. She had left the shopping bag in the kitchen. She wanted to wash out the thermos bottle before her parents came home.

Laura took the peanut butter jar out of the shopping bag. The little frog was sitting in the bottom of it. Laura wondered what the witch would do to him. Suddenly she didn't care if they ever made the witch's brew. She was going to let the frog go.

She took the jar out into the yard and set it on the ground. Then she unscrewed the lid and took it off. The

little frog hopped out of the jar. He looked around for the lake. When he didn't see it he turned and hopped back into the jar.

"Meow." Charlie had been sitting under the overhang of the bay windows to keep out of the rain. He came running to see what was in the jar.

Laura picked up the jar and screwed the lid back on. She took it back into the house.

Now Laura began to wonder what to feed the frog. There was a package of hamburger in the refrigerator. Her mother was going to use it for a meat loaf. Laura dropped a crumb of hamburger into the jar with the frog. The frog snapped it up and looked around for more.

The doorbell rang. It was Jane. "Check your list, Laura. What else do we need for the brew?" she said. "I'm tired of that witch. Let's turn her right-side-up and get rid of her."

Laura took the list out of the pocket of her jeans. It was torn and crumpled by now. And the pencil writing was blurred. "We still have to get a jelly-fish," she said. "But I don't want to make the brew." Laura told Jane how she tried to let the frog go. "I'm going to walk over to the cemetery tomorrow and turn him loose there," she finished.

"Why not use Pinky?" Jane asked.

"He's dripping wet," Laura said. "I don't think we should ride on him till he's dry."

"That means we can't go hunting jellyfish for a while either," Jane said. "It would be fun to go to the beach. Let's ask Pinky if he'd mind going in the clothes dryer. After all, your mother must have washed and dried him before."

The two girls went upstairs to the bathroom. "Pinky," Jane said, "would it hurt you to go in the clothes dryer?"

Pinky flipped one corner.

"That settles it," Laura said. "We'll just have to wait."

"Wait for what, dear?" Sally poked her head over the wall above the bath-room door.

"Jane wants to go to the beach to find a jellyfish," Laura told the witch. "But Pinky is too wet to fly."

"I wish I could remember what I did with my broom," Sally said. "It never minded being wet."

18

LAURA wanted to hide the frog before her mother and father came home. She put the jar in her dresser drawer and left the drawer open a crack to give the frog air.

After supper she made a mixture of potato peelings, onion skins, and prune pits. She took it upstairs to the witch. Sally was standing on tiptoe on the ceiling over the dresser. She was croaking.

An answering croak came from the drawer. The frog was talking to the witch.

When Laura came into the room Sally said to her, "I'm trying to explain to Tom what he has to do when we mix the brew."

"You mean he has to do something?

And nothing will be done to him?" Laura said.

"This is a cold brew," the witch reminded her. "They're hard to do. This one calls for a live frog. It would help if he were a clever frog. I picked Tom because he looked smart." She made a few more croaks and then looked to see what Laura had brought her for supper. "Lovely," she said, as she crunched a prune pit.

Laura was happy. Nothing terrible was going to happen to the frog after all. "I want to take Tom back home after we make the brew," she told Sally.

Sally was nibbling an onion skin. "Be sure to put him back in the same lake," she said. "There are five lakes in that graveyard. Laura, do you by any chance have any of those little brown things?"

Laura went back to the kitchen to get some wet coffee grounds.

19

THE next day was Saturday. Mr. and Mrs. Allen cleaned the house. Laura had to help. Pinky was still not dry. Laura was afraid her mother would put him in the dryer with the rest of the laundry. She took the bath mat out of the shower and folded him over a hanger in her closet.

Jane came to see Laura for a little while in the afternoon. "We're going to visit Granny tomorrow," she said. "I won't see you until Monday."

Laura told her about Tom.

Jane nodded. "I guess your witch isn't bad after all," she said.

On Monday Jane brought her bathing suit over to Laura's house. She went to put it on in the bathroom. "I told Mom we were going for another picnic," she said. "We could go to Coney Island, if only we didn't have to take Sally. People are sure to notice her flying around on the bottom of a bath mat."

"We could let her sit on the underside of the boardwalk," Laura said.

The witch looked through the doorway of the bathroom. "I didn't mean to listen," she said, "but I heard what you said, Jane. I know how you feel. Even right-side-up I have trouble in Coney Island. I don't mind if you go without me." Sally walked back down the ceiling of the hall to Laura's room. A minute later the girls heard her croaking to the frog.

It was easy to pack lunch when they didn't have to worry about what to feed the witch. Laura didn't want her to be hungry while they were away. She brought the kitchen garbage can upstairs and climbed on a chair to put it on the closet shelf where Sally could reach it. "Just in case you want a snack," she said.

Laura slipped out of her blue jeans and polo shirt. She put on her bathing suit. Then she took the bath mat out of the closet and into the back yard.

The yellow cat wanted to go along. He jumped into the middle of the mat and wouldn't get off. "Dogs aren't supposed to be on the beach," Jane told him. "But they always are."

"You know you don't care for swimming, Charlie," Laura reminded him.

The cat wouldn't listen. At last Laura lured him into the kitchen with a piece of chicken liver. While the cat was eating she went back into the yard and shut the door behind her.

Laura sat down beside Jane on the mat. "Please take us to Coney Island, Pinky," she said.

It was a beautiful day. Pinky flew high over the streets and houses of Brooklyn. The girls could see the ocean long before they came to Coney Island.

As they flew nearer they looked down at the beach umbrellas and the tall thrones of the lifeguards. On Monday morning the beach was less crowded than usual. Pinky dropped onto a patch

of sand in the shadow of the boardwalk. An old man was sitting on a bench at the edge of the boardwalk. He peered down at them and rubbed his eyes.

Jane and Laura stood up and stepped off the mat. Laura picked it up. Jane carried the paper bag of lunch. The girls ran across the sand.

They left the mat and the paper bag on the beach near where a fat lady was roasting herself in the sun. "I'll keep an eye on your things, children," the lady promised. She put a piece of Kleenex on her nose and rubbed suntan oil on the rest of herself.

Laura and Jane waded into the surf.

The wet sand squished between their toes. When the waves splashed them, the girls jumped into the water. Now they were wet all over. Their eyelashes and mouths were salty. It was a wonderful feeling.

Although both Jane and Laura knew how to swim, the rough waves kept knocking them back onto the beach. After a while they walked along the edge of the water. There were shells of all shapes and sizes, trailing pieces of seaweed, bits of broken plastic toys, and twisted sticks of driftwood. But they didn't see any jellyfish.

"We can look after lunch," Jane said.

The fat lady had fallen asleep. The paper bag was on the sand where they had left it. Someone had opened it to look inside. The sandwiches were still there.

But the bath mat was gone!

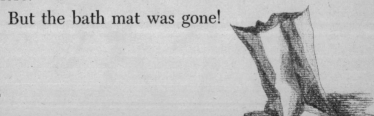

20

LAURA looked at Jane. "What do we do now?"

"I don't know," Jane said. "We don't have any money for subway fare. And we aren't even wearing shoes. It won't be much fun walking all the way home, even if we can do it."

"I'm worried about Pinky," Laura said. "The person who took him doesn't know he's magic. He'll get thrown into a washing machine and drown." Laura felt like crying. She stooped over and picked up the bag of lunch.

Jane shaded her eyes from the sun with her hand. She turned and looked all around. "Laura, look!" She pointed far down the beach.

Two big boys were strolling along,

eating hot dogs. One of them carried something pink. Jane and Laura ran after them.

By the time they caught up with the boys, both girls were out of breath. The boys had finished their hot dogs. The tallest boy had the pink thing across his shoulders now to keep off the sun.

"It looks an awful lot like Pinky," Laura whispered.

"There's one way to be sure," Jane told her. "Pinky," she called, "is it you?"

The mat waved one corner wildly.

Laura stepped in front of the boy. "That's my bath mat," she said. "Give it back."

The boy stopped walking. He looked down at her. "What are you talking about?"

"That bath mat you've got across your shoulders. It's mine." Laura held out her hand.

"It's my towel, kid. Beat it!" The boy tossed the mat to his friend. Before the other boy could catch it, Jane yelled, "Pinky, come here!"

The bath mat zoomed straight up in the air and then circled over to Jane. Laura dodged under the arm of the big boy and tore down the beach. "Come on, Pinky."

The girls raced along with the bath mat following them.

"Down, Pinky," Jane cried.

The mat came to rest on the sand. Laura and Jane ran to sit on it.

"Take us home, please," Laura said.

The bath mat rose in the air.

Jane hung her legs over the edge. "Hand me a sandwich, Laura," she said. "I'm hungry."

21

"THE best time to find jellyfish is at night." Sally sat on the ceiling of Laura's closet. The bath mat rested on the shelf below her. The witch was watching Laura and Jane clean up the closet floor. The garbage can had fallen off the shelf.

Laura dumped an apple core out of her bedroom slipper. "Maybe we can go looking for jellyfish when Mother and Daddy are asleep," she said. "But I don't think there are any at Coney Island."

Jane handed Laura a dustpan and brush. "Better sweep up those coffee grounds."

The witch clucked her tongue. "Such a waste!"

"How will we catch the jellyfish?" Laura asked.

"Just leave it to me, dear," the witch said.

Jane wiped the floor of the closet with a damp dustcloth. "I'd better go home now, Laura. I'll see you tomorrow."

"Don't you want to go jellyfishing?" Sally asked.

Jane shook her head. "My mom gets up at all hours of the night," she said. "She'd be sure to look in my room and find I wasn't there. I can't sneak out tonight. But whatever you do, don't work the spell without me."

When she went to bed that night Laura tried hard to stay awake. She heard the clock in the downstairs hall strike eleven. After that she couldn't remember anything until something brushed against her cheek. She pushed it away. Then she heard the witch's voice. "Get up, dear. Time to leave."

Laura sat up in bed. There was moonlight coming through her open window. The bath mat hovered over her bed. It was Pinky who had wakened her.

Laura got up and dressed. Pinky flew up to the ceiling so the witch could sit on his underside. Then he dropped down until he was about two feet above Laura's bed. She climbed from the bed onto the bath mat.

"Now, Pinky," Laura said, "let's see if you can find some jellyfish."

The bath mat sailed out of the window into the moonlight. He rose high in the air and flew off toward Coney Island. But before he came to the boardwalk he turned aside. He flew over an inlet. Laura looked down. She saw boats bobbing on the water below her.

"It's Sheepshead Bay," Laura said.

There were lights on the boats, but Laura couldn't see any people. The bath mat flew down until he was skimming just a foot or two above the water.

"Up a little, Pinky," the witch said. "I'm getting splashed."

The mat flew higher. Sally lay down so her head wouldn't drag in the water. Laura stared down into the depths. She could see reflections of boat lights. But there were other lights in the water — soft glowing lights that moved. One of the lights rose to the surface. Laura saw that it was like a beautiful little blue parachute. Long shining streamers

trailed behind it. Suddenly Laura knew what it was — a jellyfish.

The witch saw it too. She took off her pointed hat. "Down, Pinky!" The bath mat inched closer to the water. Sally scooped up the jellyfish in her hat. At once the hat seemed full of a raging fire. "Just calm down," the witch said to the jellyfish. "No one's going to hurt you."

Sally held out her hat. "Take it, Laura. It will be easier for you to handle."

Laura reached over the edge of the bath mat. She grabbed the hat by the brim and wedged it between her knees. It still looked as if it held a ball of fire.

Laura remembered that jellyfish sting. She was careful to keep her fingers out of the hat.

"Back to Laura's house, Pinky," the witch ordered.

The bath mat soared upward. Laura was afraid the water in the hat would spill. "Steady, Pinky, please," she said.

The sky was turning pink when the bath mat flew in Laura's open window. Sally stepped off onto the ceiling. "Don't spill the seawater, dear," she said.

Laura couldn't put the hat down. It was pointed and would fall over. She looked around her room. There was a new plastic wastebasket in the corner by her desk. Laura poured the jellyfish and the water into the wastebasket. The jellyfish blazed in anger. Laura looked to see if the wastebasket leaked. It didn't.

Sally walked into the closet and curled up on the quilt in the corner of the ceiling. "Good night, dear."

Laura folded the bath mat and put him on the shelf under the witch. She closed the closet door and dived into bed.

22

"LAURA! What's this in your waste-basket?" Mrs. Allen had come into Laura's room to wake her.

Laura sat up in bed. She blinked and rubbed her eyes. "Wastebasket?" she said. Then she remembered. "It's a jelly-fish, Mother. That's seawater in with him. Is he all right?"

"I suppose so." Her mother leaned over to look into the wastebasket. "He's glaring at me with all those little eyes he has. Laura, I never did like jellyfish. I want you to take him back where you got him."

Laura hopped out of bed. She pushed her dresser drawer shut. She wasn't sure how her mother felt about frogs. "I'll take the jellyfish back where he belongs,

Mother," she said. "I'm just taking care of him for a friend."

"Hurry and get dressed," Mrs. Allen said. "Breakfast is almost ready." She went back to the kitchen.

Jane didn't come over till the dishes were all in the dishwasher and the beds were made. Laura was beginning to worry whether she was coming at all. When the doorbell rang she ran to answer it. Jane was on the doorstep. Her face and arms seemed to be coated with pink chalk.

"What's that stuff?" Laura asked.

"Calamine lotion. I've got poison ivy." Jane said.

"But we didn't go near poison ivy," Laura said. "We're using wolfsbane in the brew instead."

"There must have been some poison ivy in the park or the cemetery. I itch something awful." Jane came into the house. "Anyway, let's get on with the spell. Did you get the jellyfish?"

Laura took Jane upstairs to look at the jellyfish. Sally was pacing around the ceiling of Laura's room. She was even more anxious than Jane to get started with the magic.

Laura shut the door of her room to keep the cat out. She got all the things for the spell ready. The buttercups and the lake water were in the closet. Sally had crunched up a piece of glass. Laura took the peanut butter jar with the frog in it out of her dresser drawer. The jellyfish was swimming angrily around in the wastebasket.

"Now," the witch said, "just how did that spell go?"

"Don't tell me you've forgotten," Jane said.

"I had it in mind only yesterday," Sally told her.

Tom was hopping up and down in the peanut butter jar. Laura took the lid off. He jumped out and grabbed the buttercups. The buttercup flowers were withered by now. Laura broke the root off. The frog grabbed the root and threw it into the jar of lake water.

"Are you sure that's a cupful?" Laura asked.

"Of course," Jane said. "Peanut butter jars have measurements marked on them. But you'd better be sure you have the right amount of ground glass."

Laura ran downstairs to the kitchen for her mother's set of measuring spoons. She looked at them. "There's no half-tablespoon here."

"Silly!" Jane said. "One tablespoon is three teaspoons."

Laura measured one and a half teaspoons of ground glass. She was about to dump it in the lake water when the witch cried out, "No, no! Make a circle on the floor with it."

"I can't," Laura said. "I'll cut my feet. Let me put down a newspaper." She went to get yesterday's paper from her parents' room. When she came back she spread the newspaper on the floor. Then she sprinkled the ground glass in a circle on the paper.

"Now shut out all the light," the witch said.

Laura and Jane pulled the cords to close the venetian blinds. The room became dusky. The girls hung blankets over the windows. Now it was really dark. The jellyfish thrashed around in the wastebasket. He gave off fiery flashes, and the green glass glittered.

The frog hopped into the center of the

ring of glass. He croaked three times. Then he leaped into the jar of lake water and fished out the buttercup root.

Tom began to jump high in the air, shaking water off the root onto the witch. She was standing on tiptoe on the ceiling.

"Take it easy, frog," Jane yelled. "You're getting me wet too."

All at once there was a crash. The witch had fallen off the ceiling.

23

LAURA ran over to the witch. "Are you hurt?" she asked.

Sally's hat had fallen off her head. She was lying quite still. Her eyes were closed. Laura bathed the old woman's forehead with lake water. Jane pulled the blankets off the windows and opened the blinds.

The frog hopped over to the witch and sat on her forehead. The old woman opened her eyes. Tom jumped down.

Sally sat up and looked around. She smiled. "It worked. I must have done the spell right." She picked up her pointed hat and jammed it over her wispy gray hair.

The frog was perched like a bird on the rim of the wastebasket. He let out a croak.

"Oh, all right, Tom," the witch said. "*You* did the spell. Now I'll have to take you home. Laura, dear," she said, "I want to ask one last favor of you."

"What is it?" Laura asked.

"Give me the bath mat," the witch said.

Laura didn't answer. She was thinking. At last she said, "If I keep Pinky, sooner or later my mother will throw him in the washing machine. He'll be better off with you."

Sally smiled. "I just remembered something," she said.

"What is it?" Jane asked.

"How I turned upside-down."

"How?" Laura wanted to know.

"I swung over the top bar of the swing set. Don't ever do it." The witch spread the bath mat on Laura's bed. Laura got a big pickle jar. She poured the seawater and the jellyfish into it. Sally set the jar on the bath mat and sat down beside it. Tom hopped onto the witch's shoulder. He croaked into her ear.

"What did he say?" Jane asked.

"He's changed his mind about going back into the pond," Sally said. "He enjoyed doing magic so much he wants to stay with me."

"You could use him," Jane said. "You're lucky we didn't get tadpoles."

The witch rubbed her chin. "You're right," she said. "In some brews you can use them instead of frogs, but I guess not in this one." She smiled.

Laura opened the window wide. "Good-bye," the witch said. "I have to take the jellyfish back to Sheepshead Bay. Thanks for everything. Come on, Pinky. Let's go."

The bath mat sailed out of the window and high over the apple tree. Jane and Laura watched until it was out of sight.

Laura folded the ground glass up in the newspaper. She threw away the buttercup plant. Jane sniffed the lake water. "Pew," she said. "Even if it still had magic in it I wouldn't use it."

Laura took the lake water into the bathroom and flushed it down the toilet.

"It's funny," Jane said. "I don't itch anymore."

Laura looked at her. "Your poison ivy seems to be cured."

"Sally said she used to be good at

granting wishes," Jane said. "And I was sure wishing I'd stop itching."

"Meow." Charlie marched into the room. He scratched at the closet door. Laura opened it.

"I'd better put that old quilt away," she said. "Sally's used it so much it's stuck to the ceiling." She went to get a chair to stand on. "I can't reach it."

Laura went down to the basement and brought back the stepladder. The cat ran up the ladder and sat down on the top step.

Jane held the ladder while Laura climbed up. She pulled at one corner of the folded quilt. Slowly the quilt unfolded and came down from the ceiling. It floated out of the closet and into Laura's bedroom. Halfway between the floor and the ceiling the quilt stopped and hung in mid-air. It seemed to be waiting for them.